WELCOME TO
PASSPORT TO READING
A beginning reader's ticket to a brand-new world!

Every book in this program is designed to build read-along and read-alone skills, level by level, through engaging and enriching stories. As the reader turns each page, he or she will become more confident with new vocabulary, sight words, and comprehension.

These PASSPORT TO READING levels will help you choose the perfect book for every reader.

READING TOGETHER
Read short words in simple sentence structures together to begin a reader's journey.

READING OUT LOUD
Encourage developing readers to sound out words in more complex stories with simple vocabulary.

READING INDEPENDENTLY
Newly independent readers gain confidence reading more complex sentences with higher word counts.

READY TO READ MORE
Readers prepare for chapter books with fewer illustrations and longer paragraphs.

This book features sight words from the educator-supported Dolch Sight Words List. This encourages the reader to recognize commonly used vocabulary words, increasing reading speed and fluency.

For more information, please visit passporttoreadingbooks.com.

Enjoy the journey!

Little, Brown and Company
Hachette Book Group
1290 Avenue of the Americas, New York, NY 10104
Visit us at LBYR.com

First Edition: September 2017

Little, Brown and Company is a division of Hachette Book Group, Inc.
The Little, Brown name and logo are trademarks of Hachette Book Group, Inc.

The publisher is not responsible for websites (or their content) that are not owned by the publisher.

LCCN 2017942058

ISBNs: 978-0-316-50928-2 (pbk.), 978-0-316-50932-9 (ebook), 978-0-316-50929-9 (ebook), 978-0-316-50931-2 (ebook)

Printed in the United States of America

CW

10 9 8 7 6 5 4 3 2 1

Passport to Reading titles are leveled by independent reviewers applying the standards developed by Irene Fountas and Gay Su Pinnell in *Matching Books to Readers: Using Leveled Books in Guided Reading*, Heinemann, 1999.

Licensed By:

TRANSFORMERS RESCUE BOTS

TRAINING ACADEMY

Welcome to the Training Academy!

Adapted by **Justus Lee**

Based on the episode
"The More Things Change" written by
Zac Atkinson *and*
"The More Things Stay the Same" written by
Brian Hohlfeld

LITTLE, BROWN AND COMPANY
New York Boston

Attention, Rescue Bots fans!
Look for these words when you read
this book. Can you spot them all?

base

track

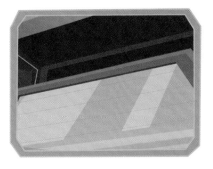

doors

buttons

The Rescue Bots have
a new Training Academy!

It will train the Bots
to be ready for any mission.

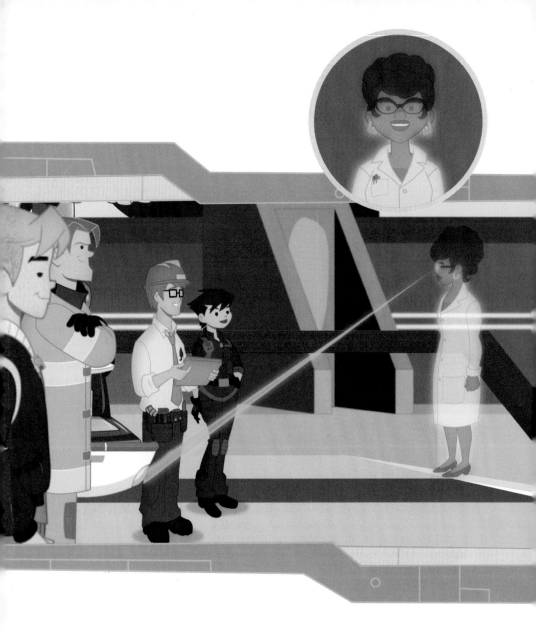

Meet Elma!

She is a hologram.

She controls everything at the new base.

The team is excited to explore.

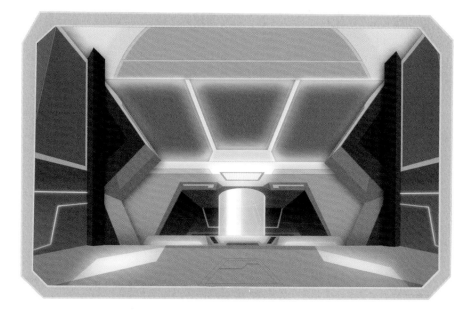

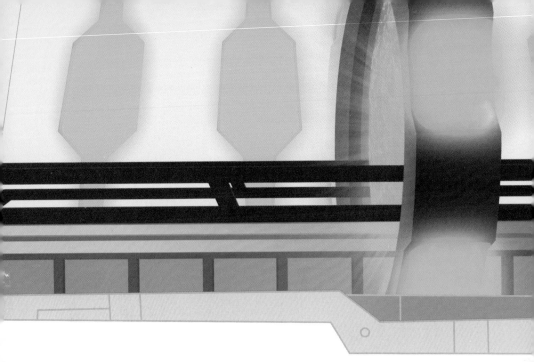

This is the ground bridge.

It makes traveling easy.

The team takes an elevator
to see the Rescue Arena.

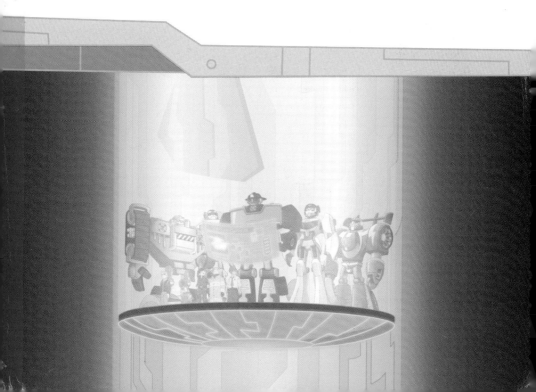

The base is big.
Cody wants to know how
the Bots hide it.

Graham knows.

Projectors make a fake image
over the academy.

The team heads over to see
Blurr's slot-car track.
Who wants to race Blurr?

Quickshadow will.

Elma shrinks the Bots.

The race is on!

Quickshadow wins!

What is that sound?

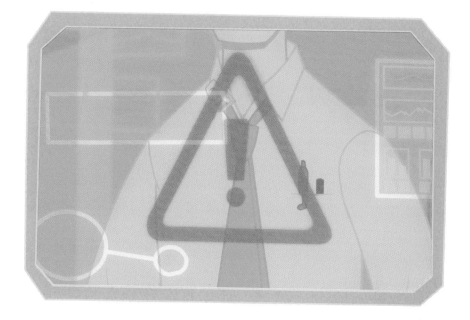

Something is happening to Elma.
She turns mean!

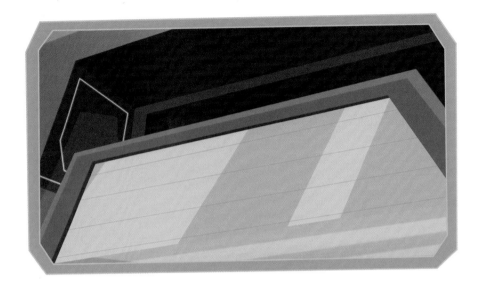

Elma locks the doors and
turns off the projectors.

The team must fix the projectors!
The real base must not be seen!

Boulder has a plan.

Blurr and Quickshadow are still small.
They can help.

The heroes form two teams.

Each team has a mission.

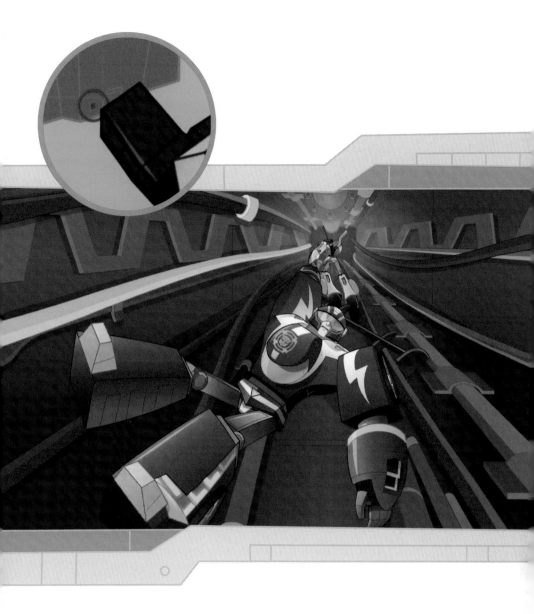

Team One climbs up to the panel.

They go outside.

Team Two goes upstairs.

Heatwave tears open the door

for Cody and Kade.

Cody and Kade reboot the system.

Elma is fixed!

The rest is up to Blurr and Quickshadow.

The Bots reach the projectors.

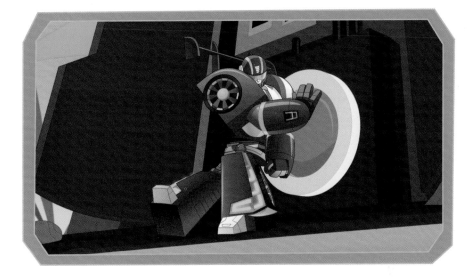

But they are too small
to push the buttons.
Quickshadow has an idea.

They change into their car modes.

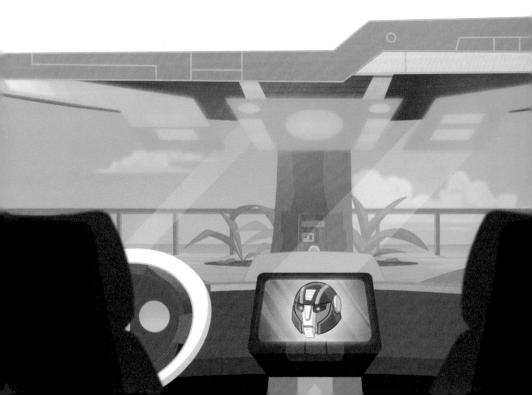

They drive as fast as they can.

They drive into the buttons.

The projectors are fixed.

The Training Academy is hidden again!

The Rescue Bots save their new home.
Good work, team!